A
COOK'S
Notebook

Design and illustrations by Cheryl A. Benner

Quotations reprinted with permission from: *Leo Rosten's Treasury of Jewish Quotations,* copyright Leo Rosten, 1972, published by Doubleday.
Crafts and Country Living, Victoria Abeles, copyright 1976 by Van Nostrand Reinhold (All rights reserved). *The New Speaker's Treasury of Wit and Wisdom* by Herbert V. Prochnow (copyright 1958), and *The Toastmaster's Treasure Chest* by Herbert V. Prochnow (copyright 1988), both Harper and Row Publishers, Inc.

Cauliflower is nothing but cabbage with a college education.
Mark Twain

Never eat more than you can lift.
Miss Piggy

If no one sees you eat it, it has no calories.

The critical period in matrimony is breakfast-time.
A.P. Herbert

There's somebody at every dinner party who eats all the celery.
Kin Hubbard

Eat to live, and not live to eat.
Benjamin Franklin

Cooking is like love. It should be entered into with abandon or not at all.

Harriet Van Horne

*Eat honey, for it is good, and the drippings of the honeycomb
are sweet to your taste.*

Proverbs

My advice to you is not to imagine why or whither, but just enjoy your ice-cream while it's on your plate—that's my philosophy.

Thornton Wilder

If you fatten up everyone around you, you'll look thinner.

Part of the secret of success in life is to eat what you like and let the food fight it out inside.

Mark Twain

I go by tummy-time and I want my dinner.
Winston Churchill

Only eat broken cookies. The process of breaking the cookies causes a calorie leakage—the smaller the broken pieces, the better. Don't forget the crumbs.

No man can be wise on an empty stomach.
George Eliot

Sustain me with raisins, refresh me with apples.
Solomon's Song

Woe to the cook whose sauce has no sting.
Chaucer

He was a very valiant man who first adventured on eating of oysters.

Thomas Fuller

Hunger finds no fault with the cookery.
Henry George Bohn

Calorie-count is one half if you and a friend both eat the same amount.

Strange to see how a good dinner and feasting reconciles everybody.

Samuel Pepys

Grub first, then ethics.
        Bertold Brecht

If you have a fine meal, enjoy it in a good light.
Talmud

Beautiful soup! Who cares for fish, game, or any other dish?
Who would not give all else for two pennyworth only of
beautiful soup?

Lewis Carroll

Many's the long night I've dreamed of cheese—toasted mostly.
                              Robert Louis Stevenson

How long does getting thin take? Pooh asked anxiously.
A.A. Milne

Cast your bread upon the waters, for you will find it after many days.

Ecclesiastes

You don't get tired of muffins, but you don't find inspiration in them.

                                        George Bernard Shaw

Snacks consumed in a movie don't count; they are a part of the entertainment.

Appetite, a universal wolf.
Shakespeare

At other people's parties, one eats heartily.
Jewish proverb

You tell me whar a man gits his corn pone, en I'll tell you what his 'pinions is.

Mark Twain

Soup and fish explain half the emotions of life.
Sydney Smith

The only emperor is the emperor of ice-cream.
                                    Wallace Stevens

And out of the ground the Lord God made to grow every tree that is pleasant to the sight and good for food.

Genesis

Nothing helps scenery like ham and eggs.
Mark Twain

*It is not really an exaggeration to say that peace and happi-
ness begin, geographically, where garlic is used in cooking.*
Marcel Boulestin

Better is a dinner of herbs where love is than a fatted ox and hatred with it.

Proverbs

Discovery of a new dish does more for human happiness than the discovery of a new star.

Anthelme Brillat-Savarin

Poets have been mysteriously silent on the subject of cheese.
G.K. Chesterton

A piece of toasted bread with sweet butter and homemade jam is an experience to be revisited.

Kim Victoria Abeles

Let my beloved come to his garden and eat its choicest fruits.
Solomon's Song

In England there are sixty different religions, but only one sauce.

Voltaire

It is not well for a man to pray, cream; and live skim milk.
Henry Ward Beecher

Behold, what I have seen to be good and fitting is to eat and drink and find enjoyment in all the toil with which one toils.
Ecclesiastes

When one has tasted watermelons, one knows what angels eat.
Mark Twain

Wish I had time for just one more bowl of chili.
(alleged) dying words of Kit Carson

If you drink a diet soda with a candy bar, they cancel each other out.

It isn't so much what's on the table that matters, as what's on the chairs.

W.S. Gilbert